TOP
SECRET
BOY STUFF

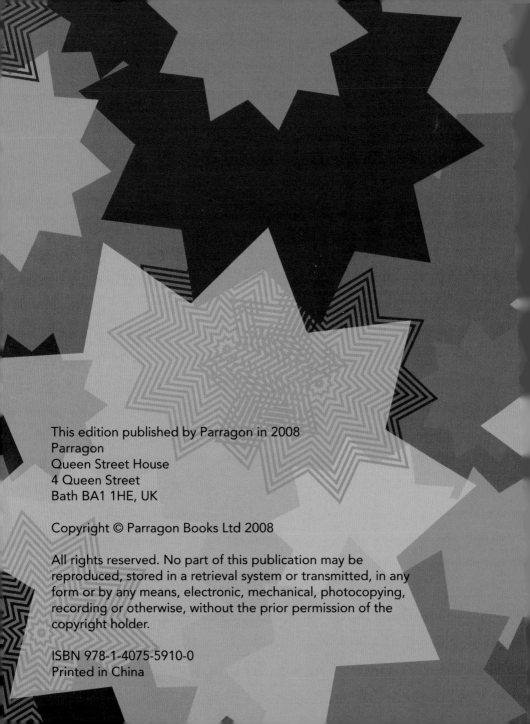

This edition published by Parragon in 2008
Parragon
Queen Street House
4 Queen Street
Bath BA1 1HE, UK

ISBN 978-1-4075-5910-0
Printed in China

TOP SECRET BOY STUFF

THIS BOOK IS ALL ABOUT ME

(and it's officially top secret)

Signed ....

Date ....

Illustrated by Dan Crisp
Written by Kirsty Neale

PaRragon

Bath · New York · Singapore · Hong Kong · Cologne · Delhi · Melbourne

IT'S ALL INSIDE!

HEY! IT'S ME!

Name: ....
....

Nickname: ....
....

Age: ....
....

Address: ....

....

Home telephone number: ....
....

....

Cell phone number: ....

E-mail: ....

8

PRINTS CHARMING

Did you know that humans and koala bears are two of the only animals who have fingerprints? Each and every fingerprint is different. Rub one of your index fingers over an ink pad. Then press it onto the white star to make your own unique mark.

DUDE ALERT!

Draw a self-portrait

THE NITTY GRITTY

My height:.......................
Eye color:. ....
Hair color:......................
Shoe size:.......................

I am......................... handed. (right/left)
My belly button is an..................... (innie/outie)
I sing like a................................ (rock star/cat)
My best feature is my...
The famous person I look most like is...............
....

SPECIAL SKILLS

	YES	NO
Rolling my tongue	✦	✦
Wiggling my ears	✦	✦
Raising my eyebrows one at a time	✦	✦
Touching my toes	✦	✦

BIGFOOT!

How to make some cool three-dimensional feet!

- Buy some sandbox sand and plaster of Paris.
- Pour the sand into a tray and add some water.
- Press your bare feet down hard into the wet sand to make prints about 1 to 1.5 inches deep.
- Follow the plaster of Paris instructions and pour some into the footprints.
- Let the plaster set for an hour, then dig out the plaster feet. You could stick them to your wall to look as if they're climbing up!

11

WELCOME TO MY ART GALLERY

All of the pictures are of.................(that's me),
and they're drawn by...................(that's me, too).

My best
portrait:

Me in
disguise:

Me as an
old man:

Me as
a girl:

It's your art. If you prefer, stick mini
photos in the frames instead of drawings,
and draw on the photos with felt-tip pens.

HI-TECH ART

You can scan art and photographs into a computer and play around with the colors. Get a computer-whiz to show you how. Then you can buy transfer computer paper and print your computer art on to it so you can iron it onto your clothes.

Me as a cartoon character:

Me first thing in the morning:

Me as modern art:

Me in a bad mood:

WORK OF A GENIUS

13

MY FAMILY

My mom's name:

....

Her real age (not the one she pretends to be):

....

My dad's name:

....

Most embarrassing thing about him:

....

BROTHERS / SISTERS

Names:

....

....

Ages:

....

....

BEST OF THE REST

My oldest relative:

....

Worst dancer in our family:

....

Relative most likely to make me laugh:

....

My favorite cousin:

....

Hairiest relative:

....

Youngest member of our family:

....

BRANCHING OUT

Try mapping your family tree.

- Start with yourself and any brothers or sisters, then move on to your mom and dad.
- Add in their brothers and sisters (your aunts and uncles), any children they have (your cousins) and then move on up to your grandparents.
- If you get stuck, ask older members of your family to help fill in the gaps. You'll be amazed at how far your tree stretches!

THE FAMILY FILES

These interviews contain previously undiscovered secrets about my family. They were conducted by an ace undercover agent (me).

Name of the person interviewed:

....

Have you ever had a nickname and, if so, what?

....

Do you have a hidden talent and, if so, what is it?

....

What present do you want for your next birthday?

....

What movie star are you most like? (yeah, right!)

....

Name of the person interviewed:

....

Have you ever had a nickname and, if so, what?

....

Do you have a hidden talent and, if so, what is it?

....

What present do you want for your next birthday?

....

What movie star are you most like? (yeah, right!)

....

Name of the person
interviewed:

....

Have you ever
had a nickname
and, if so, what?

....

Do you have a
hidden talent and,
if so, what is it?

....

What present do
you want for your
next birthday?

....

What movie star
are you most like?
(yeah, right!)

....

Name of the person
interviewed:

....

Have you ever
had a nickname
and, if so, what?

....

Do you have a
hidden talent and,
if so, what is it?

....

What present do
you want for your
next birthday?

....

What movie star
are you most like?
(yeah, right!)

....

TOP TIP: Sit opposite the person as you interview
them, so you can look into their eyes and tell
they're telling the truth. If you suspect their school
nickname wasn't really Genius, you can then
dig a bit deeper and get to the truth!

SCHOOL STAR

Name of my school:

My class teacher:

Principal:

Favorite subject:

Least favorite subject:

TEACHER WATCH

Favorite teacher:

Funniest teacher:

Strictest teacher:

Strangest teacher:

Q: WHAT'S WORSE THAN FINDING A CATERPILLAR IN YOUR SCHOOL LUNCH? A: FINDING HALF A CATERPILLAR!

Q: DID YOU HEAR ABOUT THE CROSS-EYED TEACHER?
A: SHE COULDN'T CONTROL HER PUPILS!

GEOGRAPHY GENIUS

Draw a map of your school. Use the ideas below
and number each place as you draw it on.
Then add some of your own ideas.

19

NOBODY'S BUSINESS
(BUT MINE)

My secret ambition:

Most embarrassing TV show I watch:

My worst habit:

Person I secretly think is cool:

Name I secretly wish I was called:

Cheesiest singer/band/song I always sing along to:

TOP SECRET PAGE

Most embarrassing picture of me ever

```
┌─────────────────┐
│  STICK A        │
│  PHOTO          │
│  HERE           │
└─────────────────┘
```

STAY
SECRET

If you want to keep your answers top secret, write in invisible ink, otherwise known as lemon juice!

⚙ Dip a toothpick into the lemon juice and write your answers on the page. Once the juice dries, they'll be completely invisible.

⚙ To reveal the answers later on, point a hair dryer at the page. It'll warm the lemon juice and the words will appear like magic.

STOP NOSYING NOW!

WHAT'S IN A NAME?

Work out wizard, martian, or secret spy names for your friends and family. You could use them as nicknames or code names.

Try disguising your autograph by signing with your other hand (if you're left-handed, sign with your right hand, or if you're a right-hander, do it with your left).

HOW TO WORK OUT YOUR WIZARD NAME

Use the name of a family pet for your first name. For the next part, take the first letter from your first name, move it to the end and add "o." So if Simon Simpson has a cat called Oscar, he would be Oscar Imonso.

YOUR WIZARD NAME:

....

Sign your autograph here:

....

Disguised autograph here:

....

HOW TO WORK OUT YOUR SECRET SPY NAME

Take your dad's middle name for the first part and then add the name of your street. If your dad's name was James Albert Spencer and you lived in Montgomery Avenue, you'd be called Albert Montgomery.

YOUR SECRET SPY NAME:

....

HOW TO WORK OUT YOUR MARTIAN NAME

Spell out your last name backward as the first part, and then add the last two numbers from your phone number as words. So Charlie Jones, whose phone number is 5947826 would be called Senjo Two-Six.

YOUR MARTIAN NAME:

....

DO IT YOURSELF

Try making up your own name game. You can invent a way to work out your pirate name, an action-hero name, or even a fancy upper-class name (the longer the better for this one).

ME

23

MY CREW

These pages are packed with very important info about very important people—my friends!

Name:

Nickname:

Cell phone:

E-mail:

Secret skill:

Name:

Nickname:

Cell phone:

E-mail:

Secret skill:

DID YOU KNOW?

In a lifetime, the average person spends two years on the phone. Imagine the bill!

Name:

Nickname:

Cell phone:

E-mail:

Secret skill:

Name:

Nickname:

Cell phone:

E-mail:

Secret skill:

DID YOU KNOW?

The first phone book was printed in the United States in 1878. It was one page long and contained a measly 50 names!

25

WILD THING!

My pets:

....

Names:

....

Pet I'd like to own:

....

Name I'd give it:

....

My favorite wild animal:

....

PICTURE OF MY PET, OR DREAM PET:

LOONY ZOO!

Take a notebook that's spiral bound at one side and draw a different animal on each page. Make them as big as you can. Cut each page into three even horizontal sections. Flip over the pieces of each page over to create strange new animals!

Q: How do you fit six elephants in a cookie jar?

A: Take the cookies out first.

Q: What do you get if you cross a shark with a snowball?

A: Frostbite.

- If I was an animal, I'd be a ....

- If my dad was an animal, he'd be a ....

- If my mom was an animal, she'd be a ....

DID YOU KNOW?
Camels have six eyelids, three on each eye.

DID YOU KNOW?
The bald eagle is not really bald—it has a head of pure white feathers.

27

MY PLACE

Draw a picture of your bedroom here, or stick in a photograph.

People allowed in my room:

....

People who are **BANNED!**:

....

The best thing about my bedroom:

....

The thing I'd most like to change about my room:

....

GO TO YOUR ROOM!

If you're always getting sent to your room, stop misbehaving! If that doesn't work, try making a boredom-survival kit to stash under your bed.

Here are a few things you might need:

- A shoe box (to store everything)
- Emergency snacks (mini-bags of raisins are good)
- A book or comics to read
- Notebook and pen for doodling
- A flashlight (for reading under the cover)
- A mini radio with earphones

TOP 3

My top 3
books or comics

1.

2.

3.

My top 3
movies

1.

2.

3.

My top 3
TV shows

1.

2.

3.

My top 3
classmates
1.
2.
3.

My top 3 CDs
1.
2.
3.

My top 3
....
(fill in your choice)

1.
2.
3.

31

3 TO FORGET

My bottom 3
books or comics
1.
2.
3.

My bottom 3
movies
1.
2.
3.

My bottom 3
TV shows
1.
2.
3.

My bottom 3
classmates
1.
2.
3.

My bottom 3
....
(fill in your choice)
1.
2.
3.

My bottom 3
CDs
1.
2.
3.

SPORTING STAR

My favorite sport:

My sporting hero:

The sport I'm best at playing:

My least favorite sport:

Sport I'd like to be really good at:

Sporting event I'd like to go to:

My favorite team:

Design a new uniform for your favorite team, or create your own Olympic flag...

GO FOR IT!

Get sporty and set up your own mini-Olympics at home. Events can include running or hopping races, relays, egg-and-spoon, and walking backward. You'll need a stopwatch and something to note down everyone's scores or best times. You could make special certificates or medals to present to the winners at the end.

MY TEAM

Put all the details of your favorite professional sports team here. Use your favorite team's colors to color in the players.

Team name:..

Team nickname:...................................

Team colors:.....................................

Where they play:.................................

Division:...

Trophies won:...

....

....

....

37

"YEAH!"

DREAM TEAM

Have fun describing your
fantasy football team here!

Manager:...................................

Quarterback:..............................

Center:.....................................

Guards:.....................................

Tackles:....................................

"COME ON!"   "TOUCHDOWN!"

"GOOD SAVE!"

"WE ARE THE CHAMPIONS!"

Running backs:.............................

Wide receivers:............................

Tight ends:.................................

Defensive line:............................

Linebackers:...............................

Defensive backs:.........................

"NICE TACKLE!"

"PASS!"

HALL OF FAME

Finish off each of these certificates by adding a name in the blank space.

This is to certify that

....

is a great friend.

This is to certify that

....

is the coolest person I know.

This is to certify that

....

is the funniest person I know.

40

This is to
certify that

....

is the most
helpful person
I know.

ʚ૩ঔ૩ও

This is to
certify that

....

is also a
great friend.

This is to
certify that

....

is OK,
even though
she's a girl.

This is to
certify that

....

is the
smartest
person I know.

WALL OF SHAME

This is to certify that
....
is the silliest girl I know.

This is to certify that
....
tells the worst jokes anyone has ever heard.

This is to certify that
....
is the stinkiest thing on the planet.

This is to
certify that
....
has smelly feet.

This is to
certify that
....
is the ugliest
ugly thing ever.

This is to
certify that
....
has the
wildest hair
in the universe.

This is to
certify that
....
is definitely
an alien from
another planet.

MY COOL STUFF

Make of my cell phone: ....

Favorite ringtone: ....

Favorite cell phone feature: ....

Make of my bike: ....

Make of my CD player: ....

Make of my computer: ....

Favorite computer game: ....

Favorite Web site: ....

My favorite gadget: ....

Coolest gadget in my house: ....

My top ten gadget
wish list:

1.

2.

3.

4.

5.

6.

7.

8.

9.

10.

TREASURE JAR

Label an empty screwtop jar "Coins you don't want," and put it in your room so people will see it when they come in and let you have their spare change. Store any spare coins you find in it, too. A good place to find them is down the side of furniture cushions. Eventually, your jar will fill up, and you'll find you have saved a lot toward a cool, new gadget!

GENIUS INVENTOR

Put on your thinking cap and try dreaming up some useful new inventions.

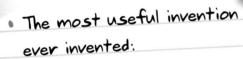

- The most useful invention ever invented:

- A really useless invention I made up:

A new type of car called

a ....

(Draw the car here)

REAL-LIFE WEIRD INVENTIONS

Chicken spectacles • Pet-stroking machine • Spider ladders (for the bath) • Motorized ice-cream cone • Knee skates • Bino-cap (a hat with built-in binoculars)

IT'S NOT JUST GADGETS AND GIZMOS THAT YOU CAN INVENT. TRY SOME OF THESE THINGS, TOO.

- A new word:...
  meaning...
- A new sport:...
  played with...
- A new name for planet Earth: ....

Drawing of my idea for an invention:

STRANGE BUT TRUE

Amaze your friends and family with these weird and wonderful facts!

BUG-TASTIC

* Butterflies taste with their feet.

* A cockroach can live for up to nine days without its head before eventually starving to death.

* Flies vomit on their food to soften it up before they start eating.

* During a lifetime, the average human will eat eight spiders while asleep.

* A honeybee has to fly 50,000 miles— that's the same as twice around the Earth—and visit 2 million flowers to make just 1 pound of honey.

* A flea can jump around 13 inches, which is around 200 times the length of its own body.

CHIEF TROUBLEMAKER

KEEP OUT!

NO ENTRY

BOYS RULE

I HATE PINK

BUZZ OFF!

ACTION HERO

HANDS OFF

YEAH, RIGHT

MY STUFF

WHAT EVER

TOP SECRET

NO THRU ZONE

BOYS RULE

I HATE PINK

NO GIRLS ALLOWED

I DIDN'T DO IT

LATER

SO?

HANDS OFF

NUMBER 1 DUDE

NO ENTRY

SNORE...

BUZZ OFF!

LET'S ROCK

DANGER ZONE

VOTE FOR ME

SUPER STAR

MY STUFF

HEY!

TOP PAL

STAY COOL

SURF'S UP

YEAH, RIGHT

NO ENTRY

LEGEND

IT WASN'T ME

ACTION HERO

BOY ON A MISSION

TOP SECRET

SAY WHAT?

IN THE ZONE

KEEP OUT!

GENIUS @ WORK

AWESOME

TOUGH ENOUGH

DO I CARE?

BOYS RULE

CHILL OUT

TOP SECRET
BOY STUFF!

DANGER
ZONE

BOYS
RULE

BOY
ON A
MISSION

TOUGH ENOUGH

NUMBER
1
DUDE

YEAH, RIGHT

SAY
WHAT?

HANDS
OFF

NO GIRLS
ALLOWED

CRAZY VEG

- They might look and taste like vegetables, but pumpkins are actually fruit. Giant pumpkins, which can weigh over 1,300 pounds, are the world's biggest fruit.

- Broccoli is also leading a double life. It's the only vegetable that is also a flower.

JUST PLAIN WEIRD

- A sneeze travels out of your nose at about 100 miles per hour.

- No piece of paper can be folded more than seven times. Try it and see!

ALL ABOUT ANIMALS

- In some countries, it's illegal to have a gorilla in the back seat of your car.

- Taking off your watch before you go swimming in the sea can help prevent shark attacks. The toothy terrors are attracted to anything that shines or glints under the water.

- Emus lay bright green eggs.

TEN COOL THINGS TO DO

Bored? Try one of these cool activities.
Check off each one after you've tried it.

1. Have a cool midnight feast.........
Invite your friends around, scrounge some tasty snacks, and dream up plenty of ghoulish ghost stories to tell each other as you eat.

2. Make your own magazine......................
Decide whether to make it a general magazine or something that's related to your hobbies and interests. You can include stories, interviews, photos, cartoons, and even competitions. It's up to you, Editor!

3. Stage a comedy show..........
Get together with a few friends and practice some jokes, silly sketches, and impressions. Make a clear space as your stage and arrange chairs around it for the audience.

4. Record a day in your life...
Grab a camera and take it with you on a normal day. Snap the places you go to and the things you do. Then stick the photos on a large piece of paper to make your very own life collage.

50

5. Google yourself.............
Ask Mom or Dad if you can use the Internet with them. Go to www.google.com and type in your name. At the top there will be a number. This is the number of times people who share your name are mentioned on the Internet across the world!

6. Start a collection..............
Ordinary things, such as stamps and postcards, are good to collect, but really strange stuff such as rubber ducks or old keys, for example, are much more fun!

7. Be a celebrity chef...........
Look in magazines or recipe books to find a recipe you'd like to try. Ask your mom or dad if you can buy the ingredients, then try it out with them as your tasters.

8. Trade your stuff..............
Everyone's got books, toys, CDs, and games they're a little bored with. Check with an adult that it's ok to trade some. Then get together with some friends who want to do the same.

9. Bury a time capsule.........
Fill a plastic box with things that represent you, your life, and the world right now. Shut the box firmly and stash it away in an attic or basement for someone (maybe even you) to discover in years to come.

10. Invent a board game.....
Dream up a board game, with a theme and rules. Then draw the board onto a big piece of cardboard and cut out playing pieces from smaller scraps.

HOW TO MAKE YOUR ROOM A GIRL-FREE ZONE

HEAD 'EM OFF

How to keep girls from entering your room:

- Make a big "keep out" sign to go on your door. Stick on some photos of creepy bugs and write: "Danger—creepy bug and spider zone."

- Tie a pair of stinky socks to the door handle.

- Fill an old yogurt or margarine container with small pebbles. Add a lid, tie a piece of string around the container, and hang it over your door handle. The minute anyone tries to sneakily open the door, you'll hear them coming.

GET 'EM OUT

How to make girls leave if they do get past the door:

⚙ Get rid of anything fluffy, or hide it. Girls are attracted to cute, fluffy, cuddly stuff.

⚙ Hide any mirrors you have, and try saying the following: "What have you done to your hair?" The girl will run off to the bathroom to check, leaving you in peace.

⚙ Fill a glass jar with twigs and leaves. Add a fake plastic spider as your "pet." For extra girl-scaring power, attach a piece of clear thread and jiggle it about to make the spider move.

TOP TIP

If an annoying girl persists in bothering you in your room, go to her room and start bothering her, instead. Either she'll get the message and ask you to leave, or you'll end up having fun with stuffed animals and dolls!

RATE IT OR HATE IT

Put a check in the box that describes how you feel about each thing.

	Really Cool	Ok	Hate it!
Sport			
Dinosaurs			
Pizza			
Girls			
Math			
Reading			
Music			
Puppies			
School			
Comics			

	Really Cool	Ok	Hate it!
Computer games			
Brussel sprouts			
Dancing			
Astronauts			
Scary movies			
Ice cream			
Bugs			
Sneakers			
Parties			
Science			

TOP TIP

Use a colored pen or pencil to check the boxes. In a year's time, come back and do it again with a different color and see if your ratings have changed.

YOUR NUMBER'S UP
THE MAGIC ANSWER

Impress people with your incredible
mind-reading math, using this cool trick.

	1	2	3
Choose a number			
↓ Add 5			
↓ Add 4			
↓ Subtract 2			
↓ Add 6			
↓ Subtract the first number you thought of			
↓ Write the answer here			

Do it yourself with three different numbers. Do you see what happens? Try the trick on your friends and family and watch them be amazed when you already know the answer!

TRICKY TRIANGLE

Can you do it? Fill each circle in with a different number from 1 to 9, so that each straight line of 4 circles adds up to 17. We've put the first one in to get you started.

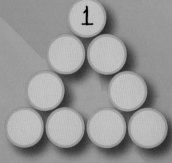

RIDDLE ME SUM-THING

1. How many months of the year have 28 days?

2. How much dirt is there in a hole 12 inches wide by 10 inches long by 16 inches deep?

MATH TEACHER: Now class, whatever I ask, I want you to all answer at once. What is six times four?

PUPILS: At once!

MATH TEACHER: If you add 34,312 + 76,188, divide the answer by 3, and times by 4, what do you get?

PUPIL: The wrong answer.

Q: Did you know there are three kinds of people?

A: Those who can count, and those who can't....

DID YOU KNOW?

There used to be a town called "6" in the United States.

ANSWERS: Tricky triangle. There is more than one way to do this. Reading clockwise, you could choose 1-6-8-2-5-7-3-9-4. Or you could try 1-6-7-3-8-4-2-5-9. Riddle me sum-thing 1) All of them have at least 28 days! 2) None—it's a hole.

COOL CAREERS

Check one answer to each question, then add up your scores to discover the job that should suit you best.

1. Which would be your favorite TV show?

- An action adventure........................ ✸
- A big sports event......................... ✸
- A comedy.................................... ✸
- ★ A cartoon................................. ✸

2. If you were a superhero, what special power would you like to have?

- Super-speed................................ ✸
- ★ Invisibility.............................. ✸
- Ability to change shape.................... ✸
- Ability to fly............................. ✸

3. Which of these school subjects are you best at?

- ★ Math..................................... ✸
- Science.................................... ✸
- English.................................... ✸
- Gym.. ✸

4. Which of these sounds like your perfect vacation?

■ A visit to Disneyland............................. ✹

● A trip into space................................ ✹

★ A visit to a big, bustling city.............. ✹

▲ A skiing trip...................................... ✹

5. What would you most like to do at the weekends?

▲ Play sport....................................... ✹

■ Go to the movie theater..................... ✹

★ Surf your favorite Web sites.............. ✹

● Visit a museum.................................. ✹

MOSTLY ▲ **S:** Energetic, enthusiastic, and determined, you'd be a fantastic sporting hero.

MOSTLY ● **S:** Adventurous, brainy, and a dreamer, you'd be a great astronaut.

MOSTLY ★ **S:** Inquisitive, alert, and smart, you'd be a great detective.

MOSTLY ■ **S:** Loud, funny, and usually the center of attention, you'd be a cool movie star.

YOU MUST BE JOKING

Q: What do you call a monster with no ears?
A: Anything you like, it can't hear you.

Q: What do you call a kangaroo at the North Pole?
A: Lost!

Q: Did you hear the joke about the garbage can?
A: It was trashy.

Q: What has a bottom at the top?
A: Your legs.

Q: Why don't lions eat clowns?
A: Because they taste funny.

Q: What's invisible and smells like banana?
A: Monkey burps.

Q: Why do elephants have so many wrinkles?
A: Because they're hard to iron.

"Doctor, Doctor, I've lost my memory."
"When did this happen?"
"When did what happen?"

Q: Why did the gum cross the road?
A: Because it was stuck to the chicken's foot.

LITTLE BOY: "Mom, people keep saying I look like a werewolf."
MOM: "Be quiet and comb your face."

Q: "Doctor, Doctor, I think I need glasses."
A: "You certainly do, Sir. This is a shoe store."

THE JOKE'S ON YOU!
Write your own favorite joke here:

61

PRANK'D
HAVE A GO AT THESE PRACTICAL JOKES!

PUT YOUR FOOT IN IT!
* To make fake dog poo, mix 1/4 cup of flour, 1/4 cup of salt, and 1/2 cup of water in a bowl.
* Roll the dough into a ball, then press the sole of a shoe into it to make a partial footprint.
* Let dry for 2—3 days, then paint it brown.
* Leave your fake dog poo lying around.

WHO NOSE?
* Secretly rub a pencil over the edges of a coin.
* Bet your victim they can't roll the coin from their forehead down to their chin without lifting it off.
* They'll do it to prove you wrong, but won't realize the special coin is leaving a smudgy line down the middle of their face.

TOE THE LINE

* Stuff some tissue into the toe of someone's shoes.
* Sit back and watch as they try to work out why they can't get their feet into a pair of shoes that fitted them perfectly yesterday.

SPOON SILLINESS

* Ask everyone at the dinner table if they can balance a spoon on their nose.
* They'll look really silly trying, but you'll do it perfectly because you know how.
* Warm the bowl (the inside) of the spoon by breathing on it.
* Tilt back your head and glide the bowl of the spoon down the bridge of your nose. Practice on your own, before you try the challenge on others.

MY MENU

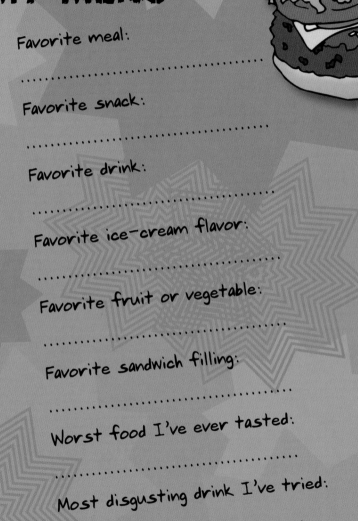

Favorite meal:

....

Favorite snack:

....

Favorite drink:

....

Favorite ice-cream flavor:

....

Favorite fruit or vegetable:

....

Favorite sandwich filling:

....

Worst food I've ever tasted:

....

Most disgusting drink I've tried:

....

GRUESOME GRUB!

BUG JUICE

- Fill an ice-cube tray halfway with water.
- Add an insect-shaped candy to each section of the tray and freeze.
- Drop your bug ice cubes into drinks and serve to unsuspecting friends.

YUMMY BRAIN CAKES

- Find a recipe for rice crispy cakes, and make them up using white chocolate.
- Add some raspberry jam to turn the mixture pink.
- Spoon oval-shaped blobs of the mixture onto wax paper to look like little brains.
- Let set before offering your "pieces of yummy brain" to friends.

DID YOU KNOW?

In some parts of the world, canned corn kernels are used as an ice-cream topping. Would you want to try it?

SECRET
SPY CLUB

Your mission, should you choose to accept it, is to get together with your friends and start a **TOP SECRET** spy club!

SECRET SIGNS

If you want to talk about your secret club or latest undercover mission, it's handy to have a way of communicating in code. Work out some secret signs with meanings that only you and your friends know. For instance, a scratch on the nose could mean: "Are you coming to the club meeting?," and a pull on the ear could mean "Yes."

NAME OF THE CLUB:

....

MY CLUB CODENAME:

....

MEMBERS:

....

....

THEIR CLUB CODENAMES:

....

....

....

66

DID YOU KNOW?

Scientists are developing super-smart digi-jewelry. A digi-necklace might really be a secret cell phone, and an innocent-looking watch could really be a mini-computer. Perfect for spies!

CLUB GOALS

What will you and your club members do? How about arranging a fund-raiser for charity, such as a sporting event between you and, say, dads, uncles, or sisters? Each player can make a small donation to take part. Here are some more ways your club could raise money for a good cause.

Turn the page to learn how you can communicate in code to keep club secrets completely hush-hush.

- Offer to do some jobs around the house for a small charity payment.

- Tell people jokes in return for a small donation.

CRACKING CODES

Try one of these cool codes to make
sure your secret messages stay secret!

EASY AS CBA

Write each word backward.
For example "this is a cool book"
becomes "siht si a looc koob."
Work out what this message says:

Lla doog seips wonk a wef tnereffid
sedoc os yeht t'nod evah ot esu eht emas
eno hcae emit.

Write your own message using this code:

....
....

ANSWERS: Backward code: All good spies know a few
different codes so they don't have to use the same one each
time. Counting code: Write your number code out on a piece of
paper for reference, but don't let it fall into enemy hands!
Alternative code: Make sure your friends know how the code
works, too, so they can read the messages you're sending.

68

COUNT ON THIS

Give each letter of the alphabet a different number, so A=1, B=2, C=3, and so on. Using this code, "it's easier than math" is "9-20-19 / 5-1-19-9-5-18 / 20-8-1-14 / 13-1-20-8-19."
Can you work out what this message says?
23-18-9-20-5 / 25-15-21-18 / 14-21-13-2-5-18 / 3-15-4-5
/ 15-21-20 / 15-14 / 1 / 16-9-5-3-5 / 15-6 / 16-1-16-5-18 /
6-15-18 / 18-5-6-5-18-5-14-3-5 / 2-21-20 / 4-15-14-20 /
12-5-20 / 9-20 / 6-1-12-12 / 9-14-20-15 / 5-14-5-13-25 /
8-1-14-4-19!
Write your own message using this code:

....

ALTERNATIVE ALPHABETS

Use every other letter to write your message, and add the alphabet in between. So "this is a great trick" is "tahbicsd iesf ag ghriejaktl tmrniocpkq."
Can you work out what this message says?
Maabkced seufrgeh yiojukrl fmrnioepnqdrss
ktnuovww hxoywz tahbec cdoedfeg whoirjkksl,
tmonoo, spoq trhsetyu cvawnx ryezaadb tchdee
mfegshsiajgkelsm ynooup'rqer ssetnudviwnxgy.
Write your own message using this code:

....

....

69

WEIRD SCIENCE

Grab your white coat and nutty professor glasses and try these cool science experiments!

MAGIC JUMPING CEREAL

- Sprinkle some puffed rice cereal onto a table, and hold a plastic spoon above it.
- Nothing happens, right? Now, rub the spoon against something woolly—a sweater, for instance.
- Hold the spoon above the cereal again, and watch the pieces jump up and cling to it! This is because you've given the spoon an electric charge by rubbing it on wool. This charge attracts the cereal pieces.

How did the scientist cut the sea in half?
With a sea saw!

CRAZY CORNSTARCH

Cornstarch is used in baking. It's a lot of fun to experiment with, too, because it does something pretty weird. Do this in a sink because it's messy!

- Put a cup of cornstarch in a bowl.
- Add water to it until it looks like thick cream.
- Pick up a handful of the liquid and squeeze it quickly.
- You'll find it becomes hard! Stop squeezing and see what happens...

How do mad scientists freshen their breath? With experi-mints!

BLACK RAINBOW

Did you know that black ink actually contains a lot of different colors? Prove it with a black, washable felt-tip pen, a plate or shallow dish, and some white circular coffee filter papers.

- Put a blob of black ink in the middle of a coffee filter paper.
- Put a drop of water in the plate and lay the filter on top for a few seconds.
- Hang the paper up to dry. The black ink will run, and rainbow colors will appear!

71

DINO HUNT!

Get your friends together to try this outdoor or indoor treasure hunt with a twist.

THINGS YOU'LL NEED

- Friends
- Some plastic dinosaur toys
- Pieces of thin cardboard (some empty cereal boxes will do)
- Pens
- Scissors
- A bag or plastic box full of treats for everyone (e.g.: bags of mini cookies or candy you can share).

BEFORE YOU START

- Draw a dinosaur egg shape onto the cardboard (to do this easily, draw around a coffee mug).
- Cut it out and use this as a template to draw and then cut out some more eggs (say 8 or 9). These are your clue cards.

72

WHAT TO DO

Plan the dinosaur hunt indoors or outdoors, depending on where you want to play. Hide the bag of treats at the end of the trail. Then work backward, writing clues on your "eggs" and leaving each one along the trail, next to a dinosaur toy. If you don't have enough toys, leave a drawing of a dinosaur or dinosaur footprint next to the clue instead.

✿ Each clue should help lead your team of friends to the next clue and finally to the treats. For example, if the treats are hidden under your bed, the final dinosaur egg clue could say "There's a sleepy dinosaur next to some treasure. Look down low!"

DID YOU KNOW?

Feeble, girly flowers outlived the dinosaurs! Scientists have discovered flower fossils that are an amazing 120 million years old. Dinosaurs died out 65 million years ago, but flowers survived.

GUESS WHAT...

Fossilized dinosaur droppings are now being used to make jewelry. When sliced and polished, the dropping looks like a semiprecious stone.

THE WORLD'S BEST EXCUSES
(HOW TO GET OUT OF JUST ABOUT ANYTHING)

WHY DON'T YOU MAKE YOUR BED?

I'm not a carpenter.

WHY DIDN'T YOU CLEAN YOUR ROOM?

I did, but there was a freak tornado.

I didn't want to disturb the wildlife.

I'm allergic to dust.

WHY DIDN'T YOU DO YOUR HOMEWORK?

I did. I just forgot to write it down.

I did but aliens stole it.

I blew my nose too hard and my brain fell out.

I was brainwashed and it went down the drain.

I don't think clearly when I'm awake.

I DIDN'T DO IT BECAUSE...
I was too busy growing.
I'm a kid. What do you expect?

WHY DIDN'T YOU TURN OFF THE LIGHTS?
I was trying to catch a rare moth.
I'm a light sleeper.

I DIDN'T DO IT...
My clone did.

WHY AREN'T YOU PAYING ATTENTION?
I did once, and it didn't pay me back.

WHY ARE YOU ALWAYS ON YOUR PHONE?
It got stuck to my head.

ACTION FILE

SURVIVAL SKILLS

Check off the skills you've got now.
Then why not see if you can
learn some of the others?

CAN YOU...	YES	NOT YET
Read a map?		
Lay a trail with sticks or pebbles?		
Whistle to signal to someone?		
Tie two different types of knot?		
Read a compass?		

MORSE CODE

Morse code is made up of dots and dashes. You can use it with a flashlight by switching it on and off quickly for a dot, or more slowly for a dash.

A .−	**B** −...	**C** −.−.	**D** −..	**E** .	**F** ..−.
G −−.	**H**	**I** ..	**J** .−−−	**K** −.−	**L** .−..
M −−	**N** −.	**O** −−−	**P** .−−.	**Q** −−.−	**R** .−.
S ...	**T** −	**U** ..−	**V** ...−	**W** .−−	**X** −..−
		Y −.−−	**Z** −−..		

IF I WERE A
ROCK STAR

Q: What's noisy and goes up and down all day? **A:** A pop star stuck in an elevator.

My stage name:

....

Instruments I'd play:

....

Band name:

....

Title of our CD:

....

Title of our biggest hit:

....

Famous bands often have logos that their fans wear on T-shirts and badges. Draw your own imaginary band logo here.

SCOOP!

All rock stars have to give interviews to newspapers and magazines. Fill in your own imaginary interview.

How many number one hits have you had?

....

Where in the world are you most popular?

....

What's the biggest audience you've ever played to?

....

Who is your biggest fan?

....

What's it like being famous around the world?

....
....
....

What's the wildest rock-star thing you've ever done?

....
....
....

Q: How do you get cool music?
A: Put your CDs in the refrigerator!

79

OUT OF THIS WORLD

His name is: ....

His home planet is called: ....

....

Person I think is most likely to

secretly be an alien: ....

....

DID YOU KNOW?

Water onboard a spacecraft is recycled from astronauts' urine. This might sound disgusting, but the recycling machines used are so good that the water they produce is cleaner than most tap water here on Earth.

DID YOU KNOW?

A white dwarf is a small but incredibly heavy kind of star.

DID YOU KNOW?

There's no gravity in space, so astronauts can sleep any way up they want. However, they have to attach themselves to a wall, bed, or seat first so they don't float off and bump into things as they snooze.

How does a barber cut the moon's hair? **E-clipse it!**

What did one shooting star say to the other? **Pleased to meteor!**

How did the rocket lose its job? **It was fired.**

81

IF I WERE A
SUPERHERO

Draw and color in
your own
superhero uniform

- Look at a few of your favorite comic strips for inspiration.
- Notice what the characters do, how they talk, and what the backgrounds are like.

CARTOON-MAN TO THE RESCUE!

Try giving your superhero his own comic strip:

- Think of a short story, dramatic event, or funny incident involving your character.
- Then break it down into a series of pictures.
- Draw each one and add speech bubbles to help explain what's happening.

TOP TIP

- Keep your drawings bold but very simple, so they're easy to recognize and not too tricky for you to draw over and over again.

IF I WERE AN EXPLORER

The place I'd most like to explore:

....

Someone I would take with me:

....

If I could go back in time I'd visit:

....

I wouldn't like to explore:

....

CHECK THE BOXES TO RATE YOUR EXPLORER SKILLS:

	Fantastic	So-so	Rubbish!
Sense of adventure			
Naturally nosy			
Don't give up easily			
Prepared to get dirty			
Good at solving puzzles			
Sharp eyes			
Happy in any kind of weather			

QUICK QUIZ

Can you match each explorer with the place they're most famous for exploring? Do some Internet or book exploring to find out!

NEIL ARMSTRONG

LEWIS AND CLARK

THE MOON

THE AMERICAS

HENRY HUDSON

CANADA

NORTH POLE

CHRISTOPHER COLUMBUS

AMERICAN FRONTIER

NORTHWEST PASSAGE

WESTERN UNITED STATES

JOHN CABOT

DANIEL BOONE

ROBERT PEARY

Why can Mount Everest hear every word you say? **Because it's covered in mountain-ears.**

MAKING MOVIES

Kind of movie I'd most like to star in:

My movie star name:

Type of character I'd play:

Person who'd be my costar:

Name of the movie:

Draw the billboard advertising poster for your movie here:

My favorite male movie character:

....

Name of the movie he was in:

....

My favorite female movie character:

....

Name of the movie she was in:

....

TRY THIS

You can try making your own mini movie.

* Dream up a short story or sketch and find some friends who'll star along with you.
* Rehearse what you're going to do, then borrow a camcorder or video phone to film it.

YUK!

The fake blood used in movies and on TV is specially made for the job and usually comes in tubes, just like paint or toothpaste. Try making your own by mixing grape juice with dish-washing liquid.

WHEN I RULE THE WORLD...

Now, decide on five things you'd ban or get rid of.

1.

2.

3.

4.

5.

Write a list of the first five rules you'd make if you were in charge.

1.

2.

3.

4.

5.

INTO THE FUTURE

What do you want your life to
be like when you grow up?
Fill in your big plans here.

Job I will have:.......................................

Country where I will live:.........................

....

Type of house I will live in:.....................

....

Hobby I will have:..................................

Car I will drive:.....................................

....

WHO'S WHO?

Fill in the name of a classmate for
each category. The classmate I think
is most likely to...

...write a book:...

...be abducted by aliens:...

...become mayor:...

...invent something amazing:......................................

...grow a long straggly beard:....................................

...become a famous artist:..

...become a sports star:..

IF I WERE A PIRATE

☠ My pirate name would be:

....

☠ People I'd have in my crew would be:

....

....

☠ Their pirate names:

....

....

☠ My ship would be called:

....

☠ The person I'd make walk the plank would be:

....

☠ The treasure I'd look for would be:

....

DRAW A MAP OF YOUR PIRATE ISLAND,
COMPLETE WITH HIDDEN TREASURE.

Q: Why couldn't the pirate play cards?

A: Because the captain was standing on the deck.

DESIGN A FLAG FOR YOUR PIRATE SHIP HERE.

BOOK AWARDS

My favorite page in this book:

....

Page I told a lie on:

....

My best drawing in this book:

....

Page I found hardest to fill in:

....

Page I'm most proud of:

....

I FINISHED THIS BOOK ON................

I WAS.............YEARS OLD

SIGNED....................................

93